For Patsy and Kaitlyn. <insert funny cat meme here>

And monstrous thanks to my editor, Catherine,
and designer, Tom, for helping Gilly set her trap. :)

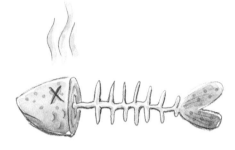

SIMON & SCHUSTER BOOKS FOR YOUNG READERS
An imprint of Simon & Schuster Children's Publishing Division
1230 Avenue of the Americas, New York, New York 10020
© 2023 by Cyndi Marko
Book design by Tom Daly © 2023 by Simon & Schuster, Inc.
For information about special discounts for bulk purchases, please contact Simon & Schuster
Special Sales at 1-866-506-1949 or business@simonandschuster.com.
The Simon & Schuster Speakers Bureau can bring authors to your live event. For more information or to book an event,
contact the Simon & Schuster Speakers Bureau at 1-866-248-3049 or visit our website at www.simonspeakers.com.
The text for this book was set in Butterfly Ball.
The illustrations for this book were rendered in watercolor and ink.
Manufactured in China
1222 SCP
First Edition
2 4 6 8 10 9 7 5 3 1
Library of Congress Cataloging-in-Publication Data
Names: Marko, Cyndi, author.
Title: Gilly's monster trap / Cyndi Marko.
Description: First edition. | New York : Simon & Schuster Books for Young Readers, [2023] | "A Paula Wiseman Book." |
Audience: Ages 4-8. | Audience: Grades 2-3. | Summary: "Gilly and her goldfish sidekick, Finnegan, set out to
trap a monster and instead wind up making a new friend"— Provided by publisher.
Identifiers: LCCN 2022007302 (print) | LCCN 2022007303 (ebook) | ISBN 9781665907552 (hardcover) | ISBN 9781665907569 (ebook)
Subjects: CYAC: Monsters—Fiction. | Goldfish—Fiction. | Friendship—Fiction. | LCGFT: Picture Books.
Classification: LCC PZ7.M33968 Gi 2023 (print) | LCC PZ7.M33968 (ebook) | DDC [E]—dc23
LC record available at https://lccn.loc.gov/2022007302
LC ebook record available at https://lccn.loc.gov/2022007303

GILLY'S MONSTER TRAP

CYNDI MARKO

A Paula Wiseman Book
Simon & Schuster Books for Young Readers
New York London Toronto Sydney New Delhi

Gilly was practically a fish.

(Everyone said so.)

Her most favorite
things were
her **FLIPPERS**.

Her best friend was a fish named
Finnegan. He had flippers too.
(Well, *fins*, but they're pretty
much the same thing.)

Gilly loved to flap her
flippers in Lighthouse Bay.

Until...

"Something swiped my woolly sweater!"

"Something pinched my pail of prawns!"

This **something** sounded serious.

"We have a monster lurking in Lighthouse Bay!" cried Gilly's brother, Gus.

Gilly flip-flapped to the beach— no monster was going to scare *her*!

FLIP FLAP

(She just hoped she didn't get eaten.)

She scanned the horizon
for horns and spikes.

She inspected the waves
for teeth and claws.

Carefully (because monsters are sneaky)

she dipped in a flipper.

"Did you see that?!
Gilly's flipper was ripped right off her foot!"

"That thing must be as big as a TANK!"

For the first time ever in the history of Lighthouse Bay, the beach was closed.

Gilly tried to flip-flap her flipper at home.

But her pool was barely a puddle.

HMMPH

And her bathtub too itty-bitty.

A visit to the market
will cheer me up, thought Gilly.

"I heard the monster nabbed a fishing net last night."

"I heard it swims underwater as fast as a TORPEDO!"

OH MY!

"Well, I heard it has teeth sharper than a SABER-TOOTHED TIGER!"

EEP!

JUMPING JELLYFISH!

"I heard its stinky breath can turn your skin GREEN!"

Gilly flopped down on the dock.

Could all the rumors be true?

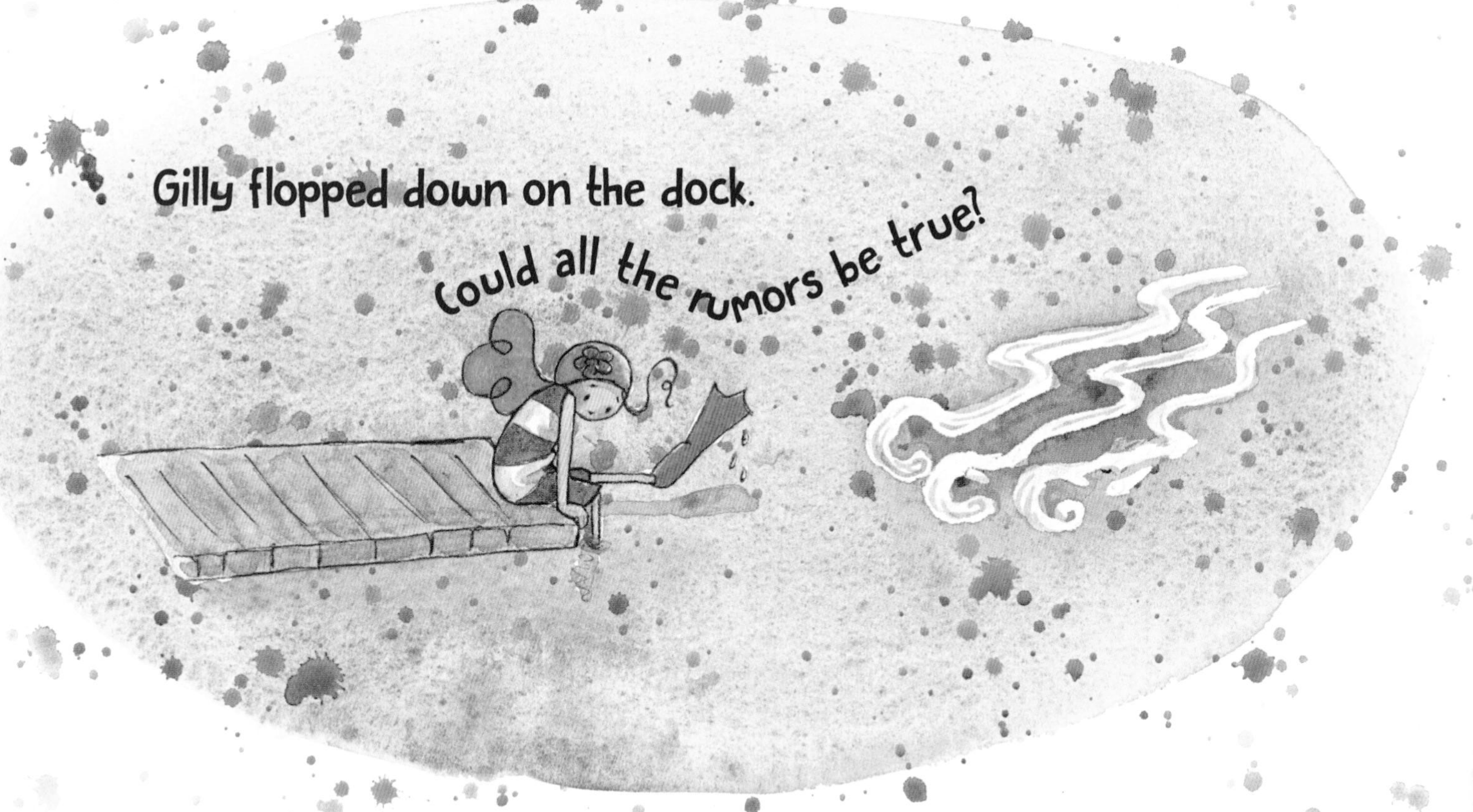

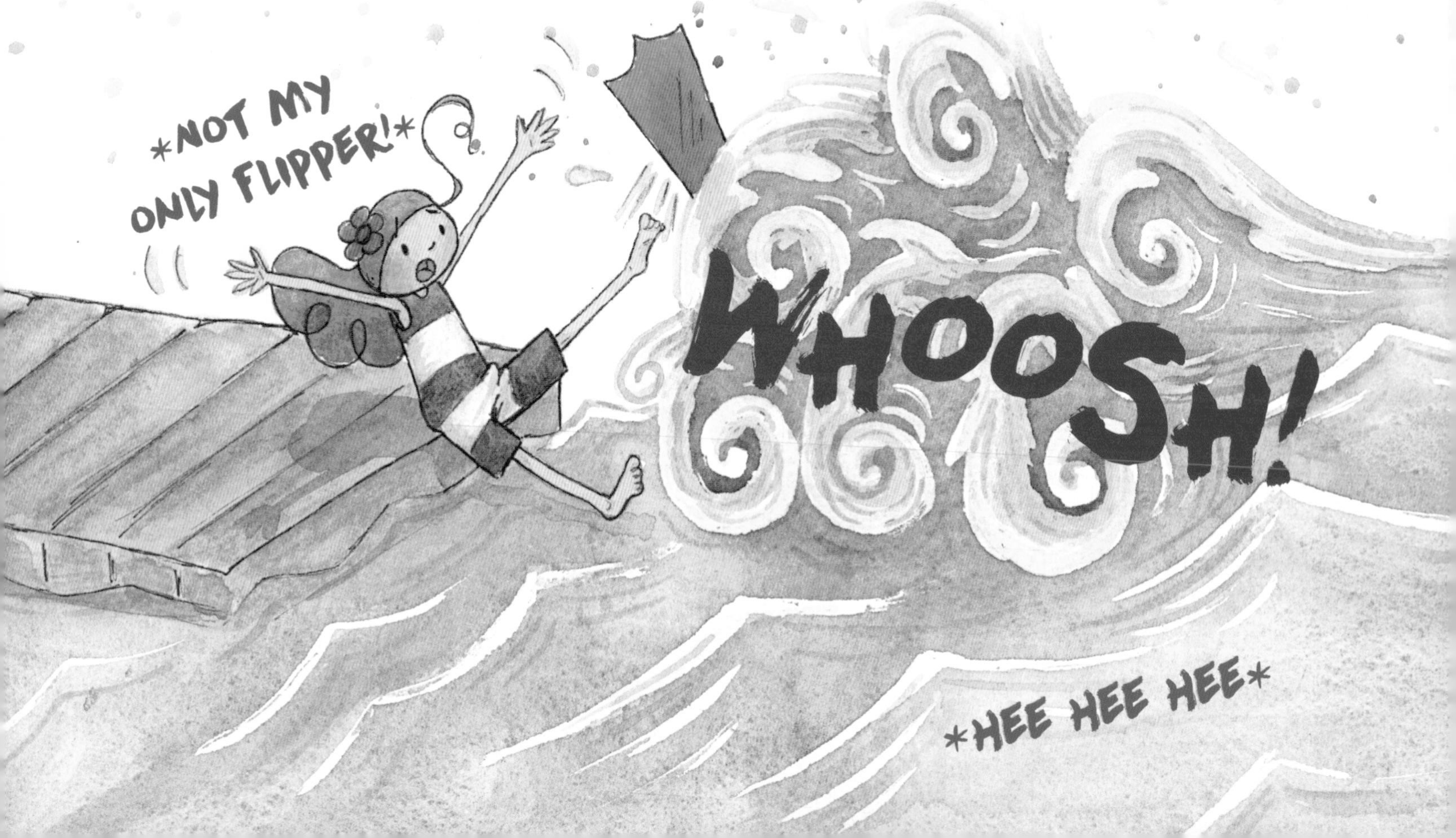

"That's it! Finnegan, I'm going to CATCH that sneaky, rotten monster and get my flippers back!" yelled Gilly.

She snatched a snack.

She hatched a plan.

"FINNEGAN, WE NEED HELP."

"DON'T WORRY, FINNEGAN. THEY WEREN'T ANYONE YOU KNEW!"

Now all they had to do was wait.

And wait…

And wait…

Until…

But *not* in Gilly's trap.

The hullabaloo was coming from the bay.

If she didn't help, it could drown!

"FINNEGAN, STAY WITH THE MONSTER! IT'S SCARED."

"Hey, marketeers!" shouted Gilly. "The monster is caught
in a net in the bay. We have to free it!"

"Why should we?" asked Gus.
"That monster is a menace!"

Gilly thought fast.

"If we don't help,
we'll *never* get
our things back!"

That did the trick.

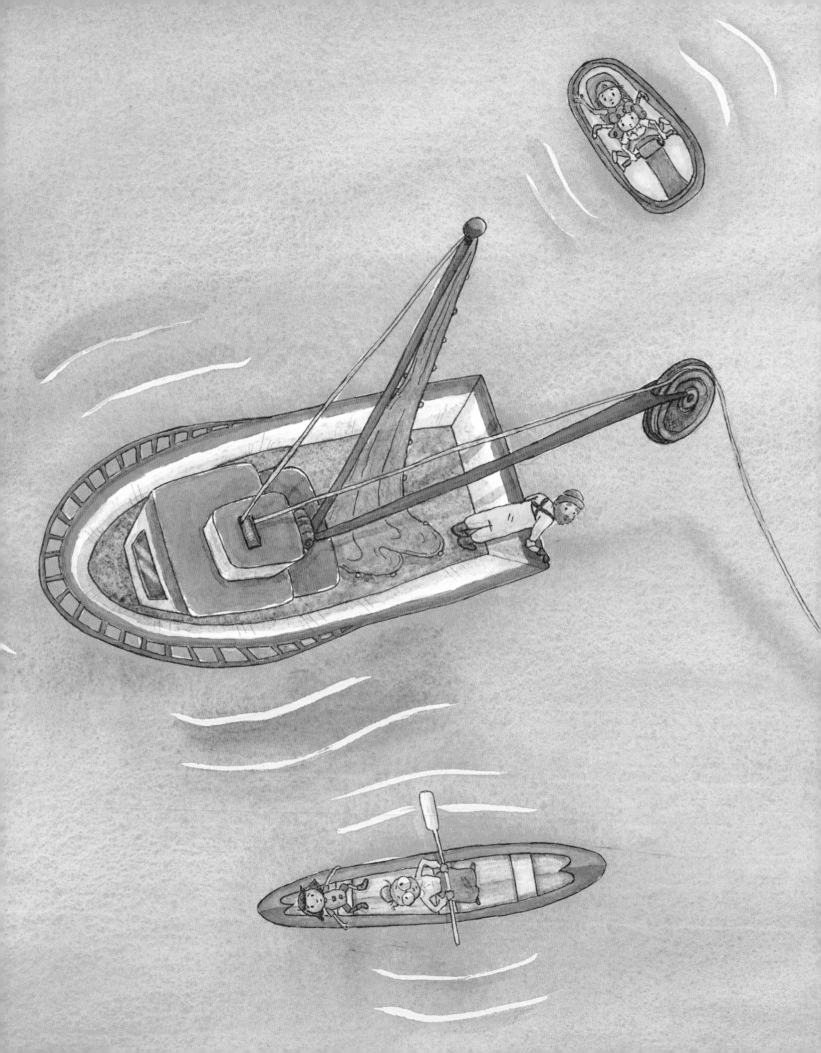

At last the monster dropped out of the net with a splash! It raced away like a blubbery submarine.

Gilly still missed her flippers,
but helping the monster felt good.

"I'M BACK, FINNEGAN!
DID YOU MISS ME?"

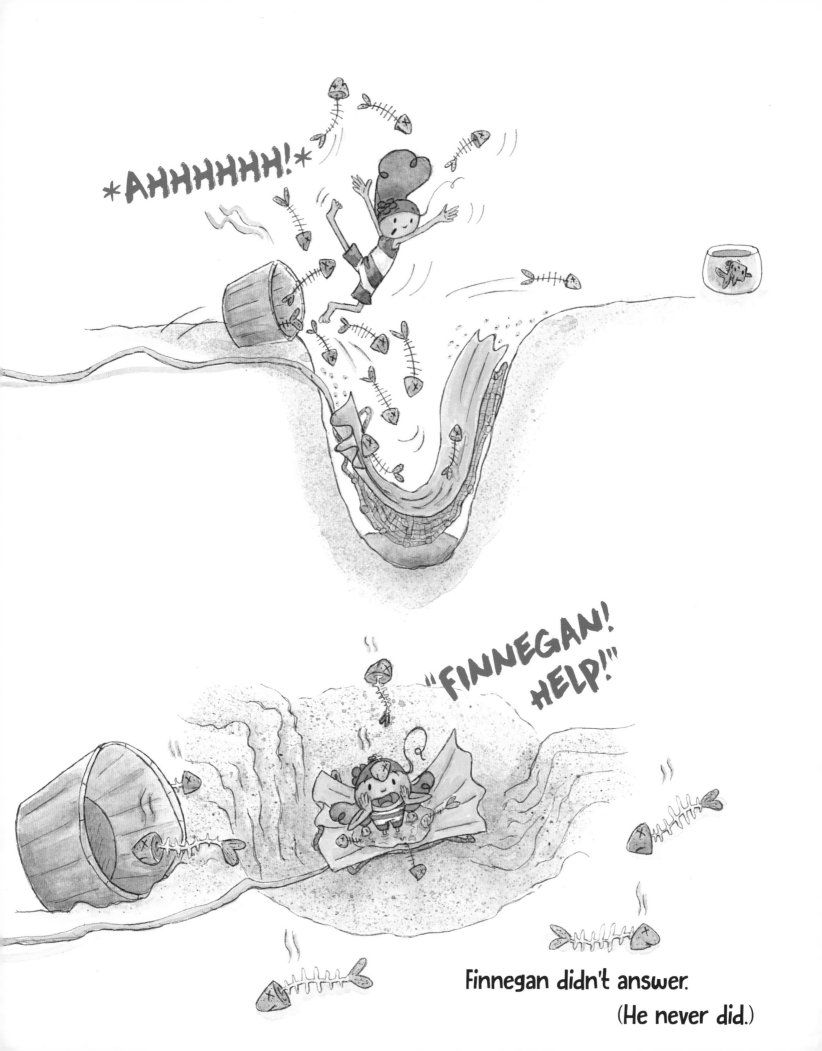

Finnegan didn't answer.

(He never did.)

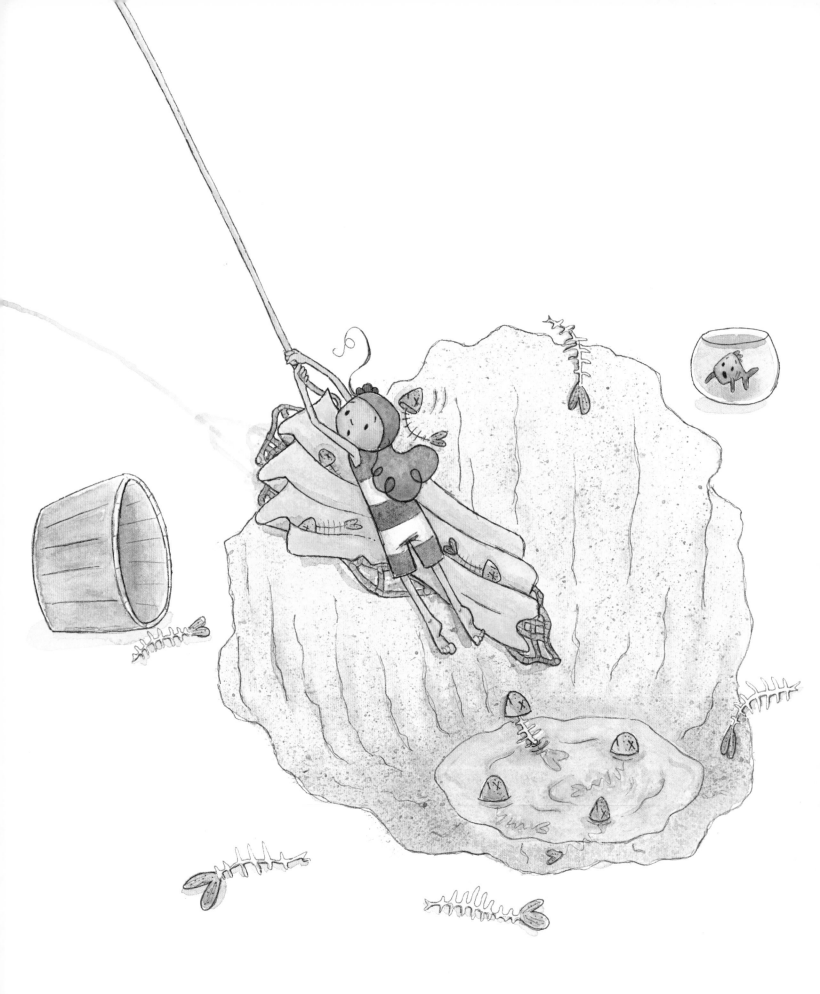

"Hey, you're not a rotten monster—
you're a sneaky walrus!"

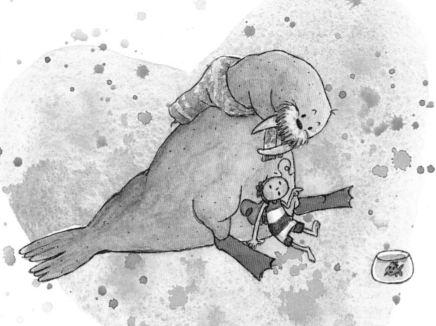

"Those are *mine*. It's not nice to take things that don't belong to you."

SPUTTER

"Oh! You have flippers too. We should be friends—I'll call you Ringo!"

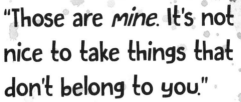

"This is our friend, Finnegan. He's not for eating."

Gilly took Ringo to meet the marketeers.

"Ringo is very sorry for borrowing our stuff without asking first," Gilly said. "He just wanted to make friends."

"To be honest, that was the most excitement we've seen around here in years," said the mayor. "Thank you, Ringo. We'd be happy to have you for a friend."

At last Gilly could flip-flap her flippers in Lighthouse Bay again.

And now that she had her new flippered friend, Ringo, to swim with, it was even more fun. Finnegan kept a close eye on them. (He always did.)

Walrus Fun Facts

Walruses are some of the largest pinnipeds (fin-footed marine mammals), second only to the elephant seal. Baby walruses weigh 100–165 pounds when they are born and can grow up to eleven feet long. Adults can weigh as much as three thousand pounds! That's the size of a small car!

The scientific name for a walrus is *Odobenus rosmarus*, which means "tooth-walking seahorse." The *Odobenus rosmarus* family is divided into two subspecies: the Pacific walrus, which is larger and more numerous, and the Atlantic walrus.

Most walruses live in the Arctic Circle. Pacific walruses live in the Bering and Chukchi Seas, and Atlantic walruses live in the Arctic Ocean, Bering Sea, James Bay, and along the Labrador coast. Haulouts are places where walruses "haul" themselves out of the water. There are haulouts of Pacific walruses in Russia and Alaska, and haulouts of Atlantic walruses in Canada, Greenland, Scandinavia, and Russia.

A prehistoric species of walrus called *Gomphotaria pugnax* that lived about six million years ago in what is now California had FOUR tusks! Two on its upper jaw, and two on its lower. Today, *Odobenus rosmarus* is the only living species of walrus, and it has just two tusks.

Walrus tusks are actually canine teeth, and they grow continually! The tusks can be up to three feet long! Walruses use their tusks to haul themselves out of the water, to cut through ice, and for defense. Males also use their tusks to show dominance. The males with the longest tusks are large and in charge!

Walruses are extreme sleepers! They can sleep for nineteen hours uninterrupted when on sea ice or land, and they can stay awake for three and a half days straight when in the ocean!

Walruses have big air sacs called pharyngeal pouches in their throats. When inflated, the pouches act as flotation devices. The walrus can then take a nap in the water, sleeping vertically, without risk of drowning. These pouches can also be used to communicate with other walruses. A walrus bellow can be heard more than half a mile away!

Walruses have big appetites! They can eat four thousand clams in one feeding! They have special whiskers called vibrissae that are full of nerve endings. They use these to help find clams and other food on the sea floor. When a walrus finds a clam, they put it to their mouth and suck the clam right out of its shell!

Walruses are fantastic divers. They can dive to a depth of almost three hundred feet and hold their breath underwater for thirty minutes. Baby walruses can also swim underwater as soon as they are born.

A group of walruses can be called a herd, a pod, or a huddle. Their herds are always separated into groups of males and females, except during mating season. Young males will stay with their mothers until they are mature enough to join a male herd.

Walruses are really social! A recent study found that walruses, especially young walruses, love to play. Walruses have been spotted sneaking up on flocks of birds, and then scaring them away.

Counting Walruses

Scientists are still learning new things about walruses because, in the past, they were hard to study in the wild. Walruses live in the Arctic Circle, and it's not an easy place to get to! Recently, the loss of arctic sea ice has made access to walrus habitats easier for scientists looking to study these awesome creatures, but it also means walruses are now threatened by loss of habitat and by humans arriving to search for oil and other resources. The World Wildlife Fund and the British Antarctic Survey started the Walrus from Space program in 2021, and each year, for five years, they aim to count every walrus on the planet! They hope the information will help find ways to protect walruses from the rapidly changing climate. Loss of sea ice as haulouts means walruses need to use more land haulouts, and more and more walruses using fewer haulouts at once can pose a risk to their safety. Walruses are sensitive, and the noise from a passing plane or ship can cause a stampede, which could lead to some walruses getting hurt. Using satellites in space to count and study walruses is more accurate and safer for the animals.

To learn more or to get involved in the count, please visit wwf.org.uk/learn/walrus-from-space.

Websites to Visit

arctickingdom.com/10-fun-facts-about-walrus/

livescience.com/27442-walrus-facts.html

wwf.ca/species/atlantic-walrus/

kids.nationalgeographic.com/animals/mammals/facts/walrus

natgeokids.com/uk/discover/animals/general-animals/walrus-facts/

seaworld.org/animals/facts/mammals/walrus/

arcticwwf.org/newsroom/the-circle/sea-change-managing-the-arctic
-ocean/monitoring-walrus-from-space-to-understand-their-plight/

mentalfloss.com/article/59266/11-rugged-facts-about-walruses

marinemammalscience.org/facts/odobenus-rosmarus/

scubadiving.com/12-interesting-facts-about-walrus

sciencealert.com/walruses-love-to-use-birds-dead-or-alive-as-toys
-scientists-observe

link.springer.com/article/10.1007/s10211-016-0248-x

wwf.org.uk/learn/walrus-from-space

macleans.ca/news/canada/could-the-walrus-return-to-the
-maritimes/

nammco.no/topics/atlantic-walrus/

adn.com/alaska-news/wildlife/2020/08/10/pacific-walrus-haulout
-near-point-lay-in-northwest-alaska-is-earliest-on-record/

fws.gov/program/alaska-marine-mammals-management-office/alaska
-walrus-program

canada.ca/en/environment-climate-change/services/species-risk
-public-registry/cosewic-assessments-status-reports/atlantic-walrus-2017.
html

polarbearscience.com/2015/08/28/pacific-walruses-hauled-out-at-point
-lay-alaska-again-this-year/